BBC
DOCTOR WHO
HOW TO BE A
TIME LORD
OFFICIAL GUIDE

POLICE PUBLIC CALL BOX   POLICE PUBLIC CALL BOX

BBC CHILDREN'S BOOKS

UK | USA | Canada | Ireland | Australia

India | New Zealand | South Africa

BBC Children's Books are published by Puffin Books, part of the Penguin Random House group of companies whose addresses can be found at global.penguinrandomhouse.com.

puffinbooks.com

 Penguin
Random House
UK

First published by Puffin Books 2014

013

Written by Craig Donaghy
Illustrations by Dan Green and Folko Streese
With thanks to Derek Handley, Peter Ware and Georgie Britton

Printed in China

A CIP catalogue record for this book is available from the British Library

ISBN: 9780723294368

BBC
DOCTOR WHO
HOW TO BE A
TIME LORD
OFFICIAL GUIDE

CONTENTS

Ahhh! There you are, Doctor! Now, maybe you've just regenerated. And maybe you haven't. But this book contains everything you need to be me! Well, you, but just like me. **This read is the only one of its kind.** Hundreds and thousands of years of Time Lord history and knowledge packed into the one book. So I've ripped out loads of pages and added my own special notes! Who wants to be any old stuffy Time Lord when you can be the Doctor?

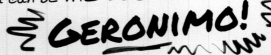

GERONIMO!

MY CERTIFICATE!

THE
TIME LORDS

The Time Lords are a hugely advanced and civilized species. We have been worshipped, respected and feared throughout the universe for millions of years. We are the leaders of the planet Gallifrey, from where we have developed the ability to travel in time using our superior technology.

Time Lords are the guardians of time. We can see everything that has been, everything that is and everything that will be. We hold the power of stars and galaxies in the palms of our hands.

THE LOCATION OF
GALLIFREY

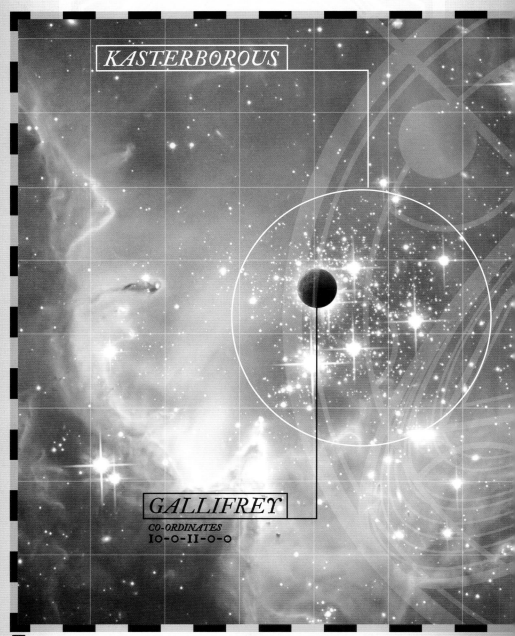

KASTERBOROUS

GALLIFREY

CO-ORDINATES
10-0-11-0-0

Gallifrey, home world of the Time Lords, is located in the constellation of Kasterborous. Its co-ordinates are 10-0-11-0-0 by 0-2 from galactic zero centre. It is also referred to, in all its glory, as the Shining World of the Seven Systems.

GALLIFREY

A GUIDE TO GALLIFREY

THE WONDROUS HOME PLANET OF THE TIME LORDS

THE CITADEL

Wild Endeavour is a key continent of the planet Gallifrey. There, within the mountains of Solace and Solitude, stands the Capitol, or the Citadel, of the Time Lords. This glorious structure is protected by a huge, transparent dome.

The twin suns of Gallifrey shine in an orange sky. Snow-capped mountains with slopes of red grass cover much of the planet's surface.

THE DEATH ZONE

This section of Gallifrey was used as an arena for fights to the death. During the Dark Times, individuals were Time Scooped and placed in the Death Zone to fight for their lives. The Tower of Rassilon is located here.

ARCADIA

Arcardia is an industrious city and home to many Gallifreyans. The planet's second city is regarded as one of the safest places on Gallifrey due to its military protection and the security of 400 sky trenches. Almost nothing in the known universe can break through these powerful airborne defences.

THE WASTELANDS

Outside the Capitol lie the desolate Wastelands. These barren lands are inhabited by primal Gallifreyans. They are content to live as savages.

TIME LORD
BIOLOGY

Externally, Time Lords look similar to a species called humans who live on the planet Earth. Time Lords, however, are far superior in every way. Here are the key differences:

Time Lords tend to live a long time and have well-developed brains, telepathic abilities and advanced memory skills.

Our respiratory bypass system allows us to exist without breathing for longer periods than other species.

A lower body temperature allows us to survive in extreme temperatures.

Blood vessels and arteries lead to two hearts. A Time Lord can survive with only one functioning heart, but it is not advisable.

Time Lords can regenerate, which will give an individual a new appearance and a new personality.

Time Lords can handle radiation that would kill humans.

HUMAN

Small brain, which is only partially used. Highly inefficient.

The average internal human body temperature is 37 degrees. This temperature can rise when fighting infection.

Two standard lungs for breathing. The left lung is smaller to allow room for the single heart.

Only one heart. This means humans are weaker and have less energy than Time Lords.

Humans can be destroyed by poisons and radiation. They must eat regularly to ensure they have energy.

That tiny heart contains lots and lots and lots of love.
For other humans, for pet dogs and for funny vegetable collections.

They're very good at making toast. They can sniff out exactly the right moment when bread is cooked to perfection.

Humans are unable to regenerate and once their life is over they simply die.

Yes, their bodies are a bit rubbish and they aren't all brainiacs like Time Lords but humans are also _amazing_!

TIME LORD
REGENERATIONS

There are many different forms of regeneration. Though each regeneration can look different, the primary purpose remains the same – to change the physical and mental form of a Time Lord, renewing him or her for a new life cycle.

THE EXPLOSION

A dramatic and instant burst of fiery regeneration energy blasts from the Time Lord.

THE WHITE LIGHT

A simple glow envelops the Time Lord, enabling the necessary change. Often takes place when a body is worn out.

THE WATCHER

The Time Lord takes the form of a mysterious, white creature – before their new appearance is finalized.

THE DISCIPLINARY

By order of the Time Lord Council, this punishment causes visions of multiple images of the Time Lord, accompanied by spinning and giddiness.

THE MEMORY VORTEX

A personal vortex appears for the Time Lord, portraying images of past loved ones and enemies.

THE SWIRL

A quick regeneration for Time Lords under attack – the face swirl is speedy and efficient.

THE MORPH

The Time Lord's body will painfully contort into its new shape, as crackles of electricity surround him or her.

THE BLUR

The Time Lord's appearance quickly blurs and their new form appears.

SEE ALSO:

THE SLOW EXPLOSION

A slower version of 'the explosion' as a gentle golden glow builds up to a dramatic burst of energy. Often found in Time Lords who are unwilling to regenerate.

THE REVERSE EXPLOSION

Whilst starting out as a huge burst of regeneration energy, this process then slows down and allows the change to take place in a quick judder.

THE TIME LORD
ACADEMY

INTRODUCTION

The Time Lord Academy is a school for training young Time Lords. At the age of eight, the brightest Gallifreyan children are chosen to attend this fine institute. It is an honour and a privilege to receive this education.

After completing a very special initiation ceremony, the new students begin their academic careers. The decades spent at the Academy teach the students about the responsibilities of being a Time Lord and ensure they receive a firm understanding of the nature and responsibility of time travel.

In order to become a Time Lord, one must successfully complete training at the Academy and swear to serve Gallifrey.

STUDENTS OF THE TIME LORD ACADEMY ARE SEPARATED INTO INDIVIDUAL HOUSES, OR 'SCHOOLS OF THOUGHT':

THE PATREX CHAPTER

- *Patrex students wear purple robes.*
- *Artists, archivists and cataloguers of information.*
- *Patrex students often display advanced telepathic abilities.*

THE ARCALIAN CHAPTER

- *Arcalian students wear green and brown robes.*

- *Solitary and logical thinkers.*

- *Arcalians have been known to excel in the field of Temporal Technology.*

THE PRYDONIAN CHAPTER

- *Prydonian students wear crimson and orange robes.*

- *Plotters, strategists and decision-makers.*

- *Prydonians are particularly skilled at languages.*

I'll give it to you straight – I was a Prydonian. That means we're supposed to be a bit cunning and sneaky! Sounds like me!

TIME LORD SYLLABUS

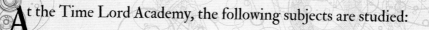

A t the Time Lord Academy, the following subjects are studied:

- Recreational Mathematics
  (including the study of Happy Prime Numbers)

- The Laws of Time

- TARDIS Maintenance

- Touch Telepathy

- Thermodynamics

- Languages

- Future History

- Transcendental
  Dimensions

- Stasis Cube Art

- Cosmic Science

BORING!

Now, here is what I think Time Lords **SHOULD** be taught in the Academy!

- How to Talk to Your **TARDIS**

- AVOIDING **EXTERMINATION**

- How to **Partially Regenerate**

- Finding the Ideal Companion

- Advanced **OOD** Management

DING!

DING!

DING!

- How to Build Things That Go **DING!**

DING!

DING!

- Coping with Post-regenerative **Wooziness**

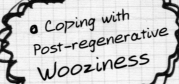

THE UNTEMPERED SCHISM

Novice Time Lords must be both brave and clever. As part of their initiation ceremony they are required to look into the Untempered Schism.

This is a gap in the fabric of reality, which allows access to the raw power and energy of the Time Vortex.

The Untempered Schism

For some young Gallifreyans, looking into the Untempered Schism can inspire them to greatness. For others, the experience is so painful and overwhelming it makes them flee, or drives them completely mad.

The Master facing the
Untempered Schism as a child

TIME LORD ACADEMY
EXAMINATION

All trainees at the Time Lord Academy must pass an exam to prove they have the knowledge and skills required to become a Time Lord. The following questions are from a standard final examination paper:

QUESTION ONE

Which star system is Gallifrey in?

A) *Kasterborous* ☐

B) *Castlebourgh* ☐

C) *Castoroil* ☐

QUESTION TWO

What does TARDIS stand for?

A) *Time And Repeated Dimension Inside Saucers* ☐

B) *Time And Relative Dimension In Space* ☐

C) *Travel and Relative Dimension in Space* ☐

QUESTION THREE

Where can you find Rassilon's Tower?

A) *The Ozone* ☐

B) *The Dead Zone* ☐

C) *The Death Zone* ☐

QUESTION FOUR

What is Gallifrey's second city called?

A) *Arcadia* ☐

B) *Tricadia* ☐

C) *The Capitol* ☐

QUESTION FIVE

What do Time Lords have that humans don't?

A) *Two eyes* ☐

B) *Two lungs* ☐

C) *Two hearts* ☐

QUESTION SIX

Where do the savages of Gallifrey live?

A) *The Citadel* ☐

B) *The Wastelands* ☐

C) *Mutter's Spiral* ☐

QUESTION SEVEN

What must novice Time Lords look into?

A) *The Untempered Vortex* ☐
B) *The Vortex Schism* ☐
C) *The Untempered Schism* ☐

QUESTION EIGHT

What is it called when Time Lords change their bodies?

A) *Restoration* ☐
B) *Regeneration* ☐
C) *Repairing* ☐

QUESTION NINE

Which of these is not a Chapter of the Time Lord Academy?

A) *Prydonian* ☐
B) *Arcalian* ☐
C) *Chameleon* ☐

QUESTION TEN

What colour are the skies over Gallifrey?

A) *Green* ☐
B) *Orange* ☐
C) *Purple* ☐

HERE ARE THE ANSWERS!

HOW DID YOU GET ON?

7C, 8B, 9C, 10B
1A, 2B, 3C, 4A, 5C, 6B,

THE TIME LORD
COUNCIL

THE RULERS OF GALLIFREY

Gallifrey is controlled by the High Council. They make the important decisions that affect Time Lords and Gallifreyans. The High Council is headed by His Supremacy, the Lord President. He is the most powerful person on Gallifrey, and therefore one of the most important beings within the entire universe.

As well as being the founder of the Time Lord civilization, Rassilon was also the Lord President. Other Presidents have included Pandak III, who held the position for nine hundred years, and Morbius who led Gallifrey into battle. He was disintegrated for his crimes.

If a Lord President is unable to name someone to succeed him, the High Council can elect a replacement. The Time Lord known as the Doctor once declared himself Lord President in order to overthrow an invasion plot. His next incarnation, the fifth, was also made Lord President, but ran away, unable to take on the heavy responsibilities of such an important role.

The High Council also includes Cardinals. They are in charge of each Chapter in the Time Lord Academy.

Another important member of the High Council is the Visionary – a Time Lord or Lady, who can predict future events.

NOTABLE TIME LORDS

RASSILON

On Gallifrey, Rassilon was the most famous Time Lord of them all. As Lord President he served his people with courage and dignity. He is regarded as the great leader of the modern civilization. Rassilon captured the Eye of Harmony – the source of Gallifrey's great power – and placed it beneath the Citadel. His remains were locked in a tomb in the Tower of Rassilon, located within the Death Zone.

Great leader? More like cruel tyrant!
The Time War changed everything - even the once noble and peaceful Time Lords. Rassilon manipulated the Master - implanting the sound of drums in his head - as a way to stop Gallifrey falling.

THE MASTER

The Master was a rogue Time Lord. He was extremely intelligent – at the Academy he achieved one of the highest degrees in Cosmic Science. But he was corrupt to his core. Some say that he went mad when he looked into the Untempered Schism as a child.

The Master worked with Autons and Cybermen as part of his diabolical schemes. He used up all of his regenerations and was executed by the Daleks on Skaro. He survived and was eventually destroyed in the Doctor's TARDIS.

BUT . . .

The Master's story didn't end there! The Time Lords brought him back to fight in the **Time War**, but he fled. He used a Chameleon Arch to hide as a human called Professor Yana.

PROFESSOR YANA

TOCLAFANE

He regenerated, stole my TARDIS and became Prime Minister of the UK. He turned the TARDIS into a **Paradox Machine** and created the **Toclafane** - cyborgs made from the last remnants of humanity. Luckily, I ruined his plans. **AGAIN!**

CRACKERS!

The Master returned. He was even **crazier** after he was resurrected. It was all part of Rassilon's plan to bring back the Time Lords. He created a world full of Masters, but in the end he did the right thing and helped me to **stop** the Time Lords.

THE RANI

The Rani is an extraordinary scientist. Although some of her techniques have been questionable, there is no doubt that she is a Time Lady of pure distinction. However, her rodent experiment resulted in the creation of giant mice that ate the Lord President's cat and justifiably led to her being exiled from Gallifrey.

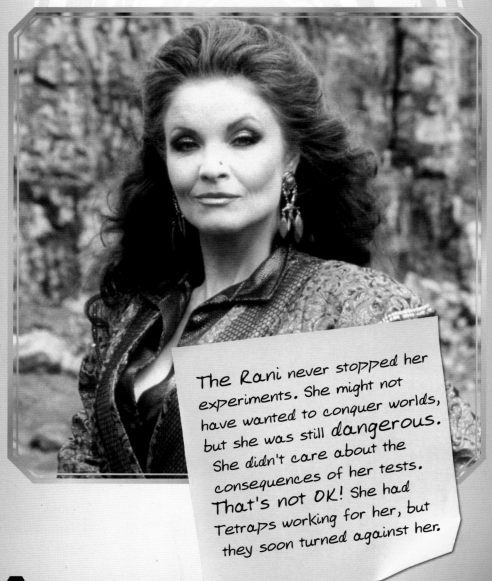

The Rani never stopped her experiments. She might not have wanted to conquer worlds, but she was still dangerous. She didn't care about the consequences of her tests. That's not OK! She had Tetraps working for her, but they soon turned against her.

THE DOCTOR

The Doctor remains one of our most complex Time Lords. Although not an academic achiever he has done many notable things. He has a unique fondness for Earth and its inhabitants. Also, he seems intent on running away – stealing a Type 40 TARDIS and exploring the universe with it. Some have labelled him 'a madman with a box'.

> Just to be clear, I am definitely a mad man with a box!

THEY **REALLY** DON'T UNDERSTAND US, DO THEY?

HERE ARE SOME OF MY RULES TO MAKE IT A LITTLE CLEARER.

1 — THE DOCTOR <u>LIES</u>.

7 — NEVER RUN WHEN YOU ARE SCARED.

27 — NEVER KNOWINGLY BE SERIOUS.

400 — YOU SHOULD ALWAYS WASTE TIME WHEN YOU DON'T HAVE ANY.

408 — TIME IS NOT THE BOSS OF YOU.

OMEGA

Omega was one of the founding fathers of the Time Lords. He created time travel with Rassilon for the people of Gallifrey by manipulating the power of stars going supernova. However, Omega disappeared when an experiment went wrong. He has not been seen since, but remains a much-revered figurehead of Gallifrey.

Don't believe everything you read! Omega was sucked into anti-matter universe where he could control everything, but only existed as thoughts. He tried to escape and take revenge on the Time Lords for abandoning him. Luckily, I was there to stop him!

WHOAH! WHOAH! WHOAH!

Now, let's not forget these special Time Lords. They might not be classed as 'notable', but they're all rather brilliant!

JENNY

She was the result of soldiers stealing my DNA to create army clones, but she had two hearts and real spirit.

That's my girl!

RIVER SONG

A child of the TARDIS, River Song (also known as Melody Pond) got all sorts of Vortex powers. She could regenerate and fly the Old Girl. Yes, she tried to kill me a few times but she also saved my life on countless occasions. One of a kind!

THE META-CRISIS ME

The result of my spare handy hand meeting some excess regeneration energy – with just a touch of human. This Doctor was a bit mouthy, but he was part Donna so that's not that surprising!

A HUMAN TIME LORD!

The result of this Meta-Crisis was pretty sad. I had to wipe Donna's memories of all our adventures, but boy, was she one smart cookie!

THE PROTECTORS OF
GALLIFREY

THE CHANCELLERY GUARD

It is the job of the Chancellery Guard to protect the Lord President, the High Council and those within the Citadel. They are responsible for all law enforcement and security.

The Leader of the Chancellery Guard is called the Castellan. Castellans have a place within the High Council, ensuring the safety and security of the Lord President at all times. Chancellery Guard Commanders report to the Castellan.

The Chancellery Guard is the only armed force within the Citadel. Members carry stasers – weapons that can stun.

CHANCELLERY GUARD RESPONSIBILITIES INCLUDE:

- *Security for important Time Lords*
- *Patrolling the Citadel*
- *Investigating crimes*
- *Interrogating suspects*

TIME WAR COUNCIL

The War Council sits apart from the High Council and the Chancellery Guard, gathering only for extreme instances or battle. They are responsible for guarding the Time Vaults, which house the forbidden weapons, and for commanding Gallifreyan armed forces.

TIME LORD HISTORY

KEY MOMENTS

Omega and Rassilon experimented with stars to produce power for time travel. Omega was lost in an anti-matter world and Rassilon became Lord President.

Time Lord intervention leads to the destruction of the Minyans on Minyos. We decide not to meddle with other planets.

 4.6 billion BC – War with the Racnoss

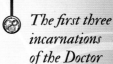 *The first three incarnations of the Doctor battle Omega.*

The First, Second, Third, Fourth and Fifth Doctors are gathered to the Death Zone as part of President Borusa's plan to gain immortality.

The Fourth Doctor becomes Time Lord President as part of a plot to defeat Vardans and a Sontaran invasion.

The Fifth Doctor is called to Gallifrey for execution, as Omega tries to connect with him.

The Fourth Doctor overthrows a plot to assassinate the Time Lord President.

Conflict with the Eternals, who banished the Carrionites into the Deep Darkness.

The Sixth Doctor is put on trial for transgressing the First Law of Time.

TARDIS GUIDE

TIME AND RELATIVE DIMENSION IN SPACE

All qualified Time Lords will know how to operate and maintain a TARDIS – a ship that can travel through space and time. The external appearance of a TARDIS can change to suit its surroundings. Though occasionally they can get stuck in a specific shape if there is a fault with the chameleon circuit.

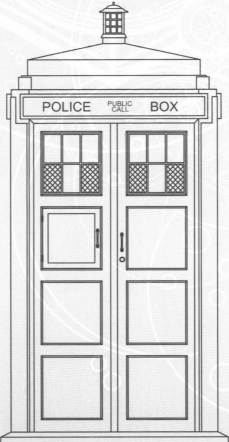

An example of a Type 40 TARDIS in the shape of a 1950s Earth police box.

For optimum performance, a TARDIS should be piloted by six Time Lords, with one positioned at each side of the console.

TARDISes must be operated with dignity and safety and should definitely not be hit with hammers. A mistake that many novices make is leaving the brakes on when landing or materializing. This creates a terrible wheezing sound.

TARDISes are created using Time Lord science. They are dimensionally transcendental, meaning they are not just bigger on the inside, but host their own dimension.

Within each TARDIS there is a section of the Eye of Harmony. The suspended decay of a star exploding and creating a black hole produces the massive energy needed to power a TARDIS.

The interior of a TARDIS can be changed according to the tastes of the owner.

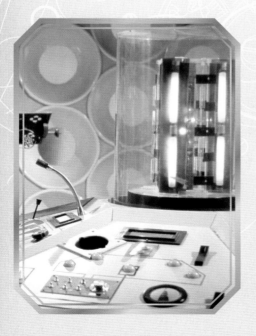

Each TARDIS holds an engine room, and an Architectural Reconfiguration System, which produces any technology that is needed. Therefore Time Lords should not feel it necessary to waste their time building their own gadgets.

All TARDISes have the same, basic capsule appearance. When the TARDIS materializes, the chameleon circuit instantly analyses a thousand-mile radius of the environment and assigns itself an appropriate disguise within nanoseconds.

A common problem with Typ

MY TOP TARDIS TIPS:

AVOID HOUSE!

This living asteroid eats TARDISes. For breakfast. For lunch. For tea. It makes me sooo mad.

GET A TOP UP!

If the TARDIS is running on empty, then you can pay a visit to Cardiff on Earth. There's a rift there where you can fill up on energy.

SOLDIER BOTHER!

So, UNIT might think they're helping out, but next time they air lift the TARDIS to safety make sure you're not in it!

THE SEAL OF
RASSILON

This is the Seal of Rassilon. It's an ancient symbol of power, and has been revered by the Time Lords throughout time.

HOW TO BE THE DOCTOR!

BY THE DOCTOR!

FOR THE DOCTOR!

Stick your face here, Doctor!

COULD ANYBODY BE MORE QUALIFIED TO TELL YOU HOW?

This is where you'll *really learn* what it's like to be a Time Lord!

INTRODUCTION

Time Lords are a proud and intelligent race . . .

BORING! BORING! BORING!

Yes, they are pretty amazing. But they also smell like dusty old books and old sprouts.

Time Lords enjoy homework and wearing big collars.

If you're going to learn how to be a Time Lord, then you're definitely going to want to be like me **or** the other versions of me.

So, I've had a bit of time on my hands lately – over **three hundred years** to be imprecise. And if I get to regenerate again, then I want me, you, to have all of the **ESSENTIAL INFORMATION** to hand. So, here's what's what and who's who:

REGENERATION

So, you've just regenerated. Ouch. Sit down and have a glass of water and some fish fingers and custard.

YOU'LL FEEL MUCH BETTER.

CLARA

She's your best friend, and you're going to need her. DO NOT mention how small her head is. For someone with a very small head she has a very big head.

ENEMIES

Yes. You have plenty. Read up on them. And then quake with fear! Or not. One or the other.

GALLIFREY

It's out there. Somewhere. Sort of.

ME/ YOU/ US

Right, Doctor, turn the page for a quick refresher on who you are/were . . .

THE FIRST DOCTOR

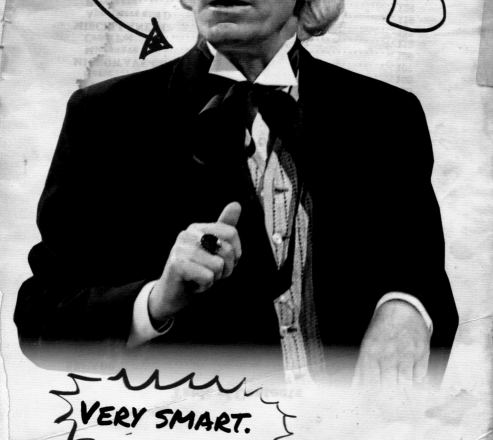

I travelled with my granddaughter, Susan.

I used to be pretty **grumpy!**

I was warm and witty, though. Some things never change.

I decided to regenerate when I got a bit tired after battling Cybermen!

45

THE SECOND DOCTOR

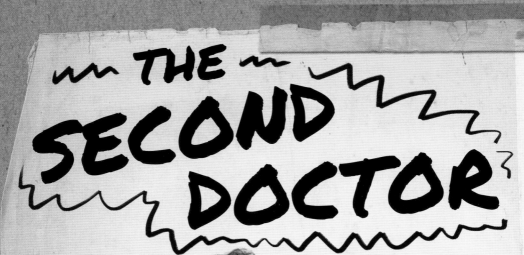

NOW, THAT'S HOW TO ROCK A BOW TIE!

BOWLS AREN'T JUST FOR CUSTARD. THEY CAN BE USED FOR HAIRSTYLES AS WELL!

HMMM, A LITTLE HOBO-ESQUE.

Everyone thought this incarnation was **much friendlier** than the last!

I was <u>cunning</u>, but I hid it well. **HOW** <u>cunning</u>.

I could also be pretty destructive – and **destroyed a few enemies.**

I was **forced** to **regenerate** as a **punishment** from the Time Lords for **meddling with time.**

Now, this version of me just loved gadgets.

I was trapped on Earth and wasn't allowed to remember how to fly the **TARDIS** (thanks for nothing, Time Lords!)

Do you remember our *Venusian Aikido* skills?

I worked for **UNIT.**

49

THE **FOURTH DOCTOR**

ONE OF MY OLD FAVOURITES, THIS FACE.

AWESOME HAT AND **CRAZY CURLS. BONUS!**

? ? ? WHAT'S THE POINT IN BEING SUBTLE? ? ? ? ?

Now, this me was **funny and clever.** Often both at the same time.

I was rather fond of **JELLY BABIES.** I even offered them to enemies!

I was pretty nifty with a **yo-yo!**

I had a pretty amazing scarf. Maybe you'll wear it? Or maybe you won't have a neck?

WHO KNOWS?

THE FIFTH DOCTOR

BACK IN THOSE DAYS
I WAS QUITE THE
CRICKET FAN.

LOVED
THIS
HAT!

CELERY —
LOOKS
GREAT
AND SAVES
LIVES.

IT TAKES A
CONFIDENT MAN
TO WEAR THESE
TROUSERS.

This was the youngest-looking me I had been until, **well, me!**

I was **very polite.** What a nice young man indeed.

Do you remember we used to say, **'brave heart'** to encourage our companions?

I was not keen on fighting.

TOO RIGHT.

I loved poetry.

And I was a stickler for proper spoken English. **YOWZAH!**

I was pretty **BOLD.** I mean look at those clothes.

THE SEVENTH DOCTOR

HATS ARE COOL. SEE!

THIS WAS MY QUESTION MARK CRAZE PHASE.

SO HANDY!

I always carried a brolly.

I think this incarnation is where I got my taste for **fezzes.**

This version of us had a Scottish accent!

!! That is probably never, ever going to happen again.

I was funny and clever, but also a bit tricksy. I gave my companion **ACE** the runaround.

THE EIGHTH DOCTOR

GOOD TO SEE THE CURLS CAME BACK.

STILL NOT GINGER, THOUGH.

VERY VELVETY!

NOT QUITE A BOW TIE, BUT GETTING THERE!

THIS OUTFIT WAS STOLEN FROM A HOSPITAL STAFFROOM.

THE CHEEK.

Ahh, look how romantic I was!

After a tricky **regeneration** it took me a while to **remember who I was.**

I tackled the **Master** and had loads of adventures.

We were so **eccentric** and **enthusiastic,** weren't we?

I tried to stay out of the **Time War** but crashing on Karn changed all that!

I learnt some good **motorbike** skills from this Doctor.

59

The Sisterhood of Karn made me realize I had to join the Time War.

? ? ? ?

I can't remember much about this version. I hope you do. He deserves that. ? ?

We chose to become this warrior.

He liked saying 'fantastic'. But, you know what, he was *fantastic*.

This guy spent a lot of time feeling **bad** about the **Time War.** Back then I didn't know what I know now.

I had a **Northern accent.**

I could be pretty **dark** or very **excitable.** How complex of me.

He travelled with Rose Tyler. **LUCKY MAN.**

THE TENTH DOCTOR

GOOD FOR LOOKING VERY CLEVER WHEN GOING 'HMMM'.

BLUE OR BROWN. WHAT A CHOICE!

THAT'S A **HANDY NEW HAND** – THE OTHER WAS CHOPPED OFF.

POCKETS ARE BIGGER ON THE INSIDE.

SAND SHOES. OH, COME ON!

Oh, this one was a right **character.** He didn't like being alone. Who can blame him?

He was _funny_ and _fast-talking_ and sometimes _unforgiving._

This was really Doctor number 11 and his spin-off meta-crisis whatsit was 12.

We had some good times and we _really_ didn't want to go.

THE ELEVENTH DOCTOR

THIS MAY OR MAY
NOT BE A WIG.

WHO KNOWS?

I WEAR A BOW TIE.

BOW TIES
ARE COOL.

JACKETS ARE SMART.
TWEEDY IS NOT
FOR THE WEEDY!

PERFECT FOR
RUNNING.

LOOK! IT'S ME!

I'm _funny_ and _bouncy_ and very _sophisticated_.

OK, I'm not that _sophisticated_. But I do like bow ties.

I've met the most _amazing people_ – the Girl Who Waited and the Impossible Girl and a version of me made out of special goo!

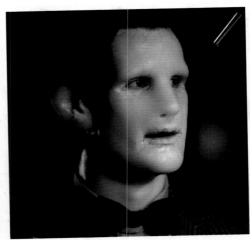

COMPANIONS

Why do you want to surround yourself with humans, robots and lizards from the dawn of time, you may ask? Because these brave, brilliant creatures will make you what you are, that's why.

You **shouldn't** be alone. That's what River Song said to me and she was right.

In order to get the best out of you, you need to travel with the best companions. Here are some things that you are definitely looking for:

COMPANIONS WITH MOTHERS WHO WILL **NOT** SLAP YOU (GOOD LUCK!)

BRAVERY

KINDNESS

A LOUD VOICE AND A BRAVE HEART

SOMEONE TO TELL YOU THAT COOL THINGS THAT ARE COOL AREN'T COOL.

A MATHS GENIUS

CLARA

Now listen, Clara is going to be your guide. She'll be sad that this face has gone, but you're going to have to look after her, so she can look after you.

CLARA IS VERY CARING. SHE LIKES LOOKING AFTER PEOPLE. BUT SHE CAN BE VERY BOSSY.

DO NOT EVER LET HER SEE THIS BOOK!

THIS IS NOT A WIG! SOME PEOPLE WEAR WIGS SOMETIMES, BUT THIS IS NOT ONE.

SHE'S GOOD AT RUNNING. WHICH MUST BE VERY HARD WITH THESE SHORT LEGS.

We have an absolute blast together. We did have. We will have. There's more about Clara on the next page! Trust me, it gets COMPLICATED.

MORE ABOUT CLARA...

THE IMPOSSIBLE GIRL

Clara isn't just any old companion. She travelled through our time stream and **broke into a million, zillion little pieces** to save all of the Doctors that have existed.

THIS IS **CLARA** WHEN SHE WAS OSWIN OSWALD.

WITHOUT HER, WE WOULDN'T BE HERE!

SADLY, OSWIN WAS TURNED INTO A DALEK. LUCKILY FOR US, SHE WAS A GOOD GUY. GOOD GAL. GOOD DALEK.

SHE LIKED MAKING SOUFFLÉS. THEY RARELY SURVIVED.

THIS IS CLARA AS, ERM, VICTORIAN CLARA.

This Clara worked as a barmaid in Victorian London and then put on a posh voice and also worked as a governess.

You might be spotting a pattern here - she just loves looking after people.

CLARA IS AN ENGLISH TEACHER. SHE WORKS AT COAL HILL SCHOOL. AHHH, NOW I REMEMBER. THAT'S WHERE OUR GRANDDAUGHTER SUSAN WENT! **REMEMBER HER?**

She's got a motorbike now. Motorbikes are **COOL.**

This is a very important leaf. It's the leaf that made Clara's mum meet Clara's dad, which is why Clara exists! I told you it was important.

71

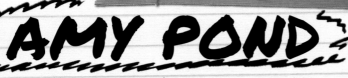

AMY POND

THE GIRL WHO WAITED WENT FROM AMELIA POND TO AMY WILLIAMS!

AMELIA POND was the first face to see this face. Whilst I sorted out the TARDIS I left her waiting for twelve years. I left her waiting on a few other occasions too, but she remained the same – brave, clever and a bit cross. When a Weeping Angel sent Rory back in time, she said goodbye to me, her **RAGGEDY MAN,** and followed Rory.

SHE LOOKED BRILLIANT AS A PIRATE QUEEN!

HER LEGS WERE TALLER THAN SHE WAS!

– A NAME RIGHT OUT OF A FAIRY TALE.

AWESOME
COMPANION TRAITS:

BRAVE – she stood up to the Daleks.

CLEVER – she built her own sonic screwdriver, sorry, probe.

STUBBORN – she followed her heart.

72

RORY POND

AHHH! Mr Rory Pond. Look at that face. That's what a hero looks like, that is. He spent nearly two thousand years as a plastic centurion guarding Amy in the Pandorica. A job well done. He grew to become a real explorer, and died a lot. **BOO.** But he came back a lot, too. **HURRAH.**

HE WAS FANTASTIC IN **PLASTIC!**

NOT A DOCTOR, BUT A NURSE!

AWESOME COMPANION TRAITS:

KIND – Rory cared about everyone.

RESILIENT – he just refused to die. Many times. Good for him.

HEROIC – he would do anything for his family.

DONNA NOBLE

THE RUNAWAY BRIDE WHO BECAME THE DOCTORDONNA

Now this one had a mouth on her! Loud as you like and brassier than brass. She wasn't just the fastest temp in Chiswick, she was compassionate, funny and always ready for adventure. A meta-crisis turned her into the **DOCTORDONNA,** but she wasn't able to keep those memories. But we will, won't we?

SHE CALLED ME SPACEMAN!
AND A FEW RUDER THINGS, TOO.

HER GRANDDAD WILF WAS PRETTY AMAZING.

AWESOME COMPANION TRAITS:

LOUD – you always knew she was coming.

COMPASSIONATE – she wanted everyone to be OK.

FUNNY – she was a brilliant mate.

MARTHA JONES

FROM WANNABE DOCTOR TO UNIT CHAMPION

Bright one, that Martha Jones. She liked me, so she must have been. Super-smart and calm in a crisis. She spent a year travelling the world on her own to help me defeat the Master. Martha went on to work for **UNIT** and then went freelance with Mickey Smith!

SHE WAS PERFECT FOR UNIT

CLEVER CLOGS

AWESOME COMPANION TRAITS:

GENIUS – a doctor AND an explorer.

LOVING – dedicated to her family.

AMBITIOUS – she was in charge of her own destiny.

CAPTAIN JACK

ROGUE TIME AGENT AND MEMBER OF TORCHWOOD

There's more to Captain Jack Harkness than being a time-hopping Time Agent from the fifty-first century. He was a hero who couldn't resist a challenge. When Rose Tyler absorbed the Time Vortex and brought him back to life, she brought him back forever! What will become of him?

FACE IN A JAR, I RECKON.

JACK WAS ONE OF MY CHILDREN OF TIME!

IS THIS JACK'S FUTURE?

AWESOME COMPANION TRAITS:

ADVENTUROUS - ready for anything!

FUNNY - he's always cracking jokes.

MYSTERIOUS - there's a lot we don't know about this guy!

ROSE TYLER

THE ORDINARY GIRL WITH AN EXTRAORDINARY LIFE

After being all Captain Grumpy, meeting Rose was magic. She was fun, adventurous, clever, kind and enthusiastic. She was just so human. She absorbed the Time Vortex to save our life and later ended up trapped in a parallel universe with a part-human Time Lord.

THIS GIRL KNEW HOW TO STAND UP TO A DALEK.

LUCKILY, THIS BAD WOLF WAS A GOOD WOMAN!

READY FOR ADVENTURE!

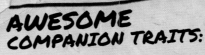

AWESOME COMPANION TRAITS:

TRUE – she was always herself.

EXCITED – she wanted to see everything and go everywhere!

BRAVE – even when she was scared she fought to be the best.

GRACE

AMAZING GRACE HELPED
ME TO STOP THE MASTER!

She was seriously clever

ACE

EVERYTHING WENT
WITH A BANG WITH
ACE – SHE MADE HER
OWN EXPLOSIVES!

Always ready for a fight

MEL

NEARLY ALWAYS SMILEY.
AND VERY SCREAMY!

Kind and bright

PERI

PERPUGILLIAM BROWN –
I REGENERATED AFTER SAVING
HER. GLAD I DID, TOO!

A keen explorer

TURLOUGH

THIS TROUBLED SCHOOLBOY WAS
SENT TO KILL ME BY THE BLACK
GUARDIAN. (HE DIDN'T!)

Determined and sharp!

KAMELION

A SHAPE-SHIFTING ROBOT. JUST WHAT
EVERYONE WANTS FOR CHRISTMAS!

Happy to serve!

ADRIC

HE WAS A TOTAL GENIUS – AND HE KNEW IT!

Brainiac

NYSSA

THIS PRINCESS WAS ALL HEART!

Caring and Kind

⸘TEGAN⸘

SHE'D HAVE GIVEN DONNA A RUN FOR HER MONEY – TALK ABOUT LOUD!

Confident and in control

ROMANA

THIS TIME LADY WAS ALWAYS ON HAND TO HELP.

Clever and bossy – then she became a little more chilled

LEELA

WAY MORE THAN JUST A SAVAGE – SHE LIKED TO LEARN

She loved a scrap!

HARRY SULLIVAN

THIS GENT WORKED FOR UNIT!

He couldn't resist a challenge

SARAH JANE SMITH

A REAL STAR – THIS JOURNALIST WAS ALWAYS CURIOUS ABOUT THE UNIVERSE

Confident and compassionate

JO GRANT

THE BRIG ASSIGNED HER TO HELP ME OUT.

Enthusiastic and resourceful

VICTORIA

SHE WAS PRETTY SMART, BUT YOWZAH, SHE COULD SCREAM!

Loud!

ZOE

THIS SUPER–SMART SCIENTIST WAS A GREAT PROBLEM–SOLVER!

Logical and brave

JAMIE McCRIMMON

THIS PIPER WAS A BRILLIANT MATE TO THE SECOND ME.

Loyal to the end

POLLY

THIS COOL GIRL FROM THE SIXTIES HELPED ME BATTLE A SUPER–COMPUTER!

Confident and dependable

BEN

He was a sailor – and very unsure of me when I regenerated!

Practical and suspicious

DODO

She reminded me of Susan!

Friendly

STEVEN TAYLOR

This space pilot was a TARDIS stowaway!

Witty and active!

VICKI

When Susan left the TARDIS I invited this girl to join me.

Bright and excitable!

BARBARA WRIGHT

Susan's teacher – but who taught whom? ✓

Saw the good in everyone!

IAN CHESTERTON

Another teacher I accidentally kidnapped. Oops! ✓

A good team player

SUSAN

My amazing granddaughter

Brilliant. Just brilliant.

RIVER SONG

Call her **RIVER SONG**, call her **MELODY POND** or call her the **IMPOSSIBLE ASTRONAUT**. Just call her – **OR YOU'LL BE SORRY!**

A BRIEF HISTORY OF RIVER SONG

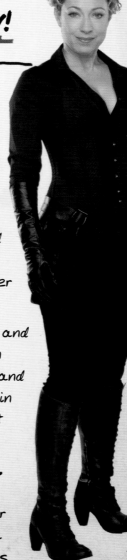

River Song is Amy and Rory's daughter. She was kidnapped by The Silence and brainwashed to kill me. She was made in the TARDIS so she has Time Lord DNA and that makes her special. She nearly killed me, but gave up her regenerations to save me.

We've had loads of adventures, and she hasn't tried to kill me in all of them! In fact, she's brave and brilliant and has the biggest, bestest hair in the galaxy. We even got married, sort of – I know, crazy!

Our lives have been very timey-wimey. The tenth me was the first incarnation to meet River, and that was at the end of her natural life. He managed to save her as a data ghost. So it's been mixed up, it's been crazy – it's been fun.

THE FACES OF RIVER SONG

MELODY POND

The astronaut kid!

MELS ZUCKER

The rebel!

RIVER SONG

The psychopath!

WARNING!

DO NOT WEAR ANY HATS IN FRONT OF RIVER SONG. SHE POKES FUN AT THEM AND ALWAYS BLASTS THEM. IT'S A SAD THING TO SEE.

THE PATERNOSTER GANG

SOME CALL THEM THE DREAM TEAM. I CALL THEM A **POTATO**, A **LIZARD** AND HER **WIFE**.

MADAME VASTRA

Vastra and her Silurian sisters were furious to be woken from hibernation by builders digging the London Underground. Vastra would have eaten them for lunch but I put her on the right track. Now, she's one of my smartest friends and advisors. She's a brilliant detective.

EATS CRIMINALS!

ARE YOU READY FOR YOUR MEDICAL?

JENNY FLINT

She's not just Madame Vastra's maid, she's her dedicated wife. And she's not just a dedicated wife, she's a fast-talking action hero. And she makes a lovely cup of tea when she isn't kicking enemy behinds!

READY FOR ACTION!

COMMANDER STRAX

He's small, he's fighty and he's <u>not the quickest of Sontarans.</u> But after becoming a nurse to humans to make amends for his naughty clone batch, Strax is one of the team. Just don't let him look after the <u>memory worm.</u>

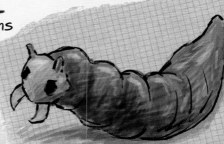

K-9

This perfect pooch was built around the year 5,000 by Professor Marius. Since then, I've knocked up a few models - including one for the wonderful Sarah Jane Smith!

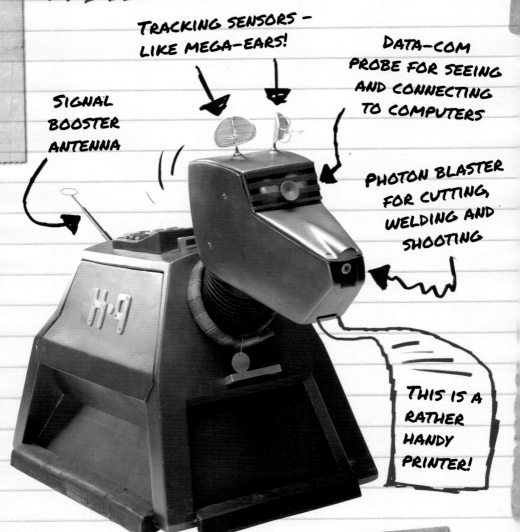

TRACKING SENSORS - LIKE MEGA-EARS!

DATA-COM PROBE FOR SEEING AND CONNECTING TO COMPUTERS

SIGNAL BOOSTER ANTENNA

PHOTON BLASTER FOR CUTTING, WELDING AND SHOOTING

THIS IS A RATHER HANDY PRINTER!

UNDERSTANDING K-9 GUIDE:

LOGIC IRREFUTABLE = YOU ARE SO RIGHT!

AFFIRMATIVE = YES!

CONFIGURED IN AGGRESSION MODE = I'M IN A GRUMP

BZZZT! = I'M DAMAGED

I WAS THINKING OF A FEW AMENDS TO FUTURE VERSIONS:

A K-9 with eight legs! Some might call it overkill, but I say give the old boy some legs, throw him a stick and watch him go.

Okay, a bit unusual, but fit him with a **microwave** and **one ear** that gives **mustard** and one that gives **ketchup**. A moving snack machine.

GENIUS!

FIND YOUR IDEAL COMPANION!

HERE'S A HANDY QUIZ TO HELP YOU WORK OUT WHAT KIND OF HELP YOU NEED!

START

How are you feeling after your regeneration?

WOOZY

Have you picked out your new outfit yet?

YES

NO

What do you fancy eating?

AN APPLE

SOMETHING DIPPED INTO SOMETHING

HUMAN

Perfect for when you're getting carried away. Listen to your human and be kind and caring. Don't start eating chips and watching loads of telly, though.

NON-HUMAN

Good choice. You need a companion with special skills – be that a lizardy tongue or a genius mathsy brain. Just make sure that they're friendly.

YES

Are you moody?

NO

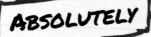

ABSOLUTELY

Can you tell if fun is important to you?

ROBOT

If you're a bit impatient then you should definitely get a robot. They're fast and efficient and only need an occasional oiling.

NOT AT ALL

NEVER LEAVE THE TARDIS WITHOUT . . .

JAMMIE DODGER

Would you risk it for a biscuit? This looks like a TARDIS self-destruct button. Well, just tell monsters that's what it is, in case they try anything funny.

SONIC SCREWDRIVER

You'll need this ALL of the time. Unless it's for something wooden – and then you should just get an axe or something.

TARDIS KEY

Important for getting into the TARDIS and summoning the TARDIS in case you end up losing it. I've NEVER done that. OK, just once or twice . . .

FEZ

Now, you'll definitely need a hat at some point for some occasion. I recommend this. Look at that beautiful tassel.

PSYCHIC PAPER

Think it and it appears – you can use this paper to trick your way in anywhere. Just don't think of a lie too big, such as 'I'm a responsible adult.'

GLASSES

Whether you need them or not, sometimes you're going to have to persuade people you're very clever.

OTHER HANDY THINGS TO CARRY: LEMON DROPS, A SMALL PLASTIC DOLL, A YO-YO, A SNOWGLOBE, CHIPMUNK REPELLENT AND HAT REPAIR KIT.

PROTECTION

ENEMIES OF THE TIME LORDS!

OK, this is the most important thing you have to read (yes, even more important than how to eat fish fingers and custard properly). **KNOW YOUR ENEMIES** - and how to run from them!

Most of the creatures in this guide aren't just enemies of me, you, us, but of **EVERYTHING IN THE UNIVERSE!** That's just not cool. You will definitely need to stop them.

SHARP TEETH ARE NATURE'S WAY OF SAYING 'I'M GOING TO GET ALL BITEY!'

SHARP CLAWS AND POINTY PAWS ARE THINGS TO STEER CLEAR OF.

BEADY EYES! TOTALLY CREEPY. AND THOSE MEAN, DOWNWARD-POINTING EYEBROWS. THEY MEAN TROUBLE.

Some things that look all **sweet** and nice really **aren't.** If you're in a regeneration daze, you might get confused and try to stroke one. **PLEASE DON'T.**

NOT CUTE ALERT!

ADIPOSE

Adorable, right? **Wrong!** They're made out of body fat. And sometimes, when things go wrong, they're made up of the churned skin, bone and hair of humans! Bleurgh!

CYBERMAT

That's not a metal rat – it's a Cybermat! Again, looks fun and sort of squeaky, but it's got nasty nipping gnashers and works for the Cybermen.

PARASITE

Ahhh, this little guy just wants a cuddle. **NO!** It's a parasite that wants to connect to you and then produce loads of poison. No cuddles for you, mister.

DALEKS

OUR GREATEST ENEMY. EVER. SOMETIMES YOU CAN'T EVEN RUN FROM THEM.

NAME: Daleks   FROM: Skaro

Created by mad genius **DAVROS** during their war with the Thals, these metal monsters have a squashy Kaled mutant inside. All they know is hate – and they want everything that is non-Dalek **EXTERMINATED.**

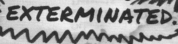

THEY CAN FLY! AND GET UP STAIRS. →

WATCH OUT FOR:

There are new Daleks in town. And by new I mean old. They're pure and powerful AND very colourful.

WEAKNESS:
Their eyestalk is their weakest point. Try bashing that if you've turned out brave.

LOOK OUT!
- THIS IS WHERE THEY SHOOT FROM.

Don't mistake the Manipulator Arm for a sink plunger. It can literally suck all the moisture out of your body!

CYBERMEN

THEY WANT TO UPGRADE HUMANITY. DON'T LET THEM, OK!

NAME: Cybermen
FROM: Mondas and Parallel Earth

There are different versions of these **steel terrors**, but they all want to **delete anything they can't upgrade**. They use humanoid body parts to build their cyborg armies and do not like emotions!

WEAKNESS:

Overloading their emotional inhibitors can make their heads **POP**. Or some gold can do **real damage**.

WATCH OUT FOR:

Cybermen with a C on their chest are from a Parallel Earth and constructed by Cybus Industries. If they're around, the walls between realities are fading.

THIS HEAD ALONE CAN BE A DANGEROUS WEAPON - WITH WHIPPY WIRES AND A SNAPPY FACE.

THEY CAN BLAST YOU WITH LASERS OR JUST ELECTROCUTE YOU!

WEEPING ANGELS

NAME: Weeping Angels
FROM: Somewhere very old

DON'T BLINK! THEY CAN'T MOVE IF YOU'RE LOOKING AT THEM.

They're quantum-locked, so they can only move when you're **NOT** looking at them. It makes blinking a real problem. If they touch you, they blast you into the past and use the power from the potential life you would have lived. Some say that's kind. I don't.

WATCH OUT FOR:

Sorry, I didn't think this through . . . images of Weeping Angels can become Weeping Angels, so watch out!

100

THEY'RE NOT CRYING, THEY JUST DO THIS SO THEY DON'T LOOK AT EACH OTHER BY ACCIDENT.

CAN THEY FLY? I HAVEN'T SEEN IT.

WEAKNESS:

I've already said it – don't blink and they won't move.

THE SILENTS

NAME: Silents
FROM: The Papal Mainframe

The Silence was a religious movement that wanted to **stop the Time War** from returning. These spooky creatures were once confessional priests that were modified so people wouldn't remember telling them their sins. They're not all bad, but they are all ugly.

WATCH OUT FOR:

Some people thought these telepathic monsters were powerless in water. Now that was a silly mistake.

WHEN THEIR MOUTH IS OPEN, THEY'RE ABSORBING ELECTRICITY TO SHOOT!

THEY CAN MAKE HUMANS POP BY BLASTING THEM WITH THEIR FINGERS!

WEAKNESS:
An eye drive was created to make them memory-proof. It was designed by them, so do be careful.

SONTARANS

NAME: Sontarans   FROM: Sontar

A CLONE RACE, BUILT FOR WAR. **SMALL BUT DEADLY.**

They might look like potatoes, but these surly little clones are bred for one purpose - **WAR.** They love nothing more than a good scrap, and being destroyed in battle is a great honour. Sounds a bit stupid, if you ask me.

WATCH OUT FOR:

Sontarans can use their cloning technology to create doubles of humans, like they did with Martha! You can recognise them by their awful smell!

PONG!!

SILURIANS

NAME: Silurians   FROM: Earth

Remember, Silurians are not aliens - they're from Earth. Some would argue they were here first so they should have it back. Wake one up from hibernation and you're likely to get blasted with a Heat Ray. So best to leave them be, huh?

WATCH OUT FOR:

Their tongues are like poisonous whips - accurate and deadly. Stay clear!

ICE WARRIORS

PROUD WARRIORS WITH IMPRESSIVE ARMOUR

Reptilian warriors inside robotic armour. Although they're big and strong they rely on their biomechanical armour and believe it is dishonourable to take it off. The suits have built-in weaponry and organic wires that can access other machinery.

NAME: Ice Warriors
FROM: Mars

WATCH OUT FOR:

Some Ice Warriors will leave their armour if it helps them escape, just like Grand Marshal Skaldak here.

ZYGONS

NAME: Zygons
FROM: Zygor

THESE SHAPE-SHIFTERS ARE ALWAYS UP TO NO GOOD!

You can't miss a Zygon - they're orange and covered in gross suckers! Most of their plans involve 'body-printing' which is a fancy word for taking humans prisoner and then copying their image. They use organic technology that is very clever, but also very slimy.

WATCH OUT FOR:

They've stolen Time Lord tech and have been hiding out in paintings. Clever old things!

Spot the Zygon!

OTHER MONSTERS TO WATCH OUT FOR:

JUDOON

These guys work for the Shadow Proclamation (boring galactic law agency). They're sort of rhino police thugs. They tend to blast first and ask questions later, so keep out of their way!

OOD

Everyone loves an Ood. They love cleaning and carrying out all of those boring tasks. But when they've got red-eye it means something bad has happened and that they'd like to zap you.

WHISPER MEN

Creepy! They're a part of the Great Intelligence. They're made out of paper and like to talk in rhymes. It's like they love being sinister!

SNOWMEN

You're bound to meet a lot of friendly snowmen, but these chaps – with the sharp icy teeth and the hunger for flesh – are not great. Keep your cool and imagine them melting, and they should turn to slush.

PEG-DOLLS

They might just say they want to play, but their Tenza-powered touch can turn you into a wooden weirdo just like them. Not a good look.

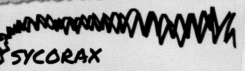

SYCORAX

Nasty things. Big into slavery and blood control. One chopped my hand off. Cheeky. Challenge their leader to a duel and send them packing.

HOW TO RUN!

You might think running is easy – wrong! It's not just putting one foot in front of the other and moving forward (OK, so technically it is), but here are my top tips for escaping danger!

THE BASIC RUN

Put one foot in front of the other, move forward and – see, I told you there was more – occasionally look back in horror to see if you're about to get eaten or exploded.

TURN AND CHECK ON HORROR!

KEEP THOSE KNEES UP!

THE HELPFUL RUN

Run, as above, but check on your companion. They're ALWAYS getting into trouble, and you'll have to help. Try grabbing their hand and screaming 'RUN! WE'RE GOING TO DIE!' to motivate them.

COME ALONG YOU!

DOCTOR, HELP!

CUSHIONS

THE SPACE RUN

Like running, but in a space suit. Put one foot in front of the other and move your arms about as you fall through the sky and hopefully land on a pile of cushions.

THE WOOZY WALK →

OK, so if you've just regenerated then it will be pretty tricky moving in a straight line. I found it tough – but running in a wibbly line is perfect for evading enemy fire!

LASERS

BLAST

FEZ →

ARGH! RUN!

THE DRUNK GIRAFFE

This isn't just an amazing and original dance. Running and waving your arms in the air is perfect for scaring away monkeys or medium-sized predators!

THE MEGA-FAST RUN

A bit unconventional this one, but wear roller skates and a super-modern jetpack. Running will never be an issue again. Stopping, on the other hand, will be problematic.

GERONIMO!

DOCTOR EXERCISES!

FEELING A BIT TIRED AND ACHEY FROM YOUR REGENERATION? THEN YOU'RE GOING TO NEED SOME SPECIAL EXERCISES!

THE CHEST STRETCH

Put those arms out and really stretch that chest. You don't want to hear any ribs *pop*, but you want to give both of those hearts a good work out!

THE SQUAT

Legs! They've always been important to me. So, you want to make sure they're as supple and flexible as possible. Bend them a few times to get them limber!

THE HEAD TILT

If you ever find yourself having to wear one of those big old Time Lord collars, or any hats that are slightly heavier than a deluxe fez, you'll need a strong neck.

HAT'S THE WAY TO DO IT!

JUMPING JACKS

Jump up in the air
several times, waving
your arms and legs.
Imagine you're fighting
off a werewolf –

IT'S VERY MOTIVATING!

I'M FLYING!

THE FORWARD ROLL

Get into a ball and then roll
forward several times. I like
to turn the gravity off in the
TARDIS first, so I can float
around like a dainty asteroid.

THE JAW

You might be blessed with a
big chin. If you are, you'll
need to maintain its firmness
by exercising. Do this one
hundred times a day.

THINGS <u>NOT</u> TO SAY TO HUMANS

If you're like the rest of us you'll be spending a <u>lot of time</u> on <u>Earth</u>. It's a <u>great planet</u>, but you'll have to learn to handle the humans.

THEY'RE VERY SENSITIVE.

WOW, YOU'VE GOT A BIG FACE!

DID YOU GET **BORED** AND SHAVE ALL OF YOUR **HAIR OFF?**

THAT'S A LOVELY SHADE OF ORANGE. HAVE YOU BEEN TAKING SKINCARE TIPS FROM A SONTARAN CLONE BATCH?

CAN I BORROW YOUR HAIR? I NEED TO DISGUISE MYSELF AS A **SHEEP.**

YOU'VE GOT THE PERFECT FIGURE TO BE MADE INTO A HUMAN SKIN SUIT FOR THE **SLITHEEN.**

ARE THEY EARRINGS OR ARE YOU SCANNING THE AREA FOR ALIEN LIFEFORMS?

I'VE JUST SAVED THE GALAXY FROM EXTINCTION BY A RACE OF ROBOT BEETLES – WHAT DO YOU MEAN YOU CAN'T GIVE ME A FREE ICE CREAM?

YOU'VE REDECORATED YOUR FACE. I DON'T LIKE IT.

IS YOUR CHIN TRYING TO HAVE AN ARGUMENT WITH YOUR NOSE? OR DO YOU NATURALLY HAVE A HEAD SHAPED LIKE A CASHEW NUT?

OOH, WHO TOOK YOUR HANDBAG?

SORRY, YOUR MAJESTY. IT'S JUST THAT HATS LOOK BETTER ON ME. OH, YOUR CROWN, YOU SAY . . .

SORRY, SORRY . . . I SOMETIMES GET CONFUSED BETWEEN HUMANS AND SOFAS. YOU'RE VERY COMFORTABLE, THOUGH.

YOU TELL ME WHICH EVIL SCIENTIST DID THIS TO YOU AND I'LL REPORT THEM TO THE SHADOW PROCLAMATION.

I NEVER KNEW BUILDERS COULD HAVE SUCH TEENY, TINY HANDS.

ALL ABOUT UNIT!

I'm sure you know that guns just make silly people even sillier, but this army might have to help you out every now and again!

OK, first things first. I did work for UNIT once. Well, what else was I going to do? I was trapped on Earth - bored out of my brain - and banned from using my blue box!

UNIT stands for Unified Intelligence Taskforce. They're top secret and guard the Earth against alien attacks. Which, as we know, happen only too often!

This is Alistair Gordon Lethbridge-Stewart, or, as we called him, the Brigadier, a.k.a. the Brig. The Brig was no-nonsense and very, very brave. He kept me in check. Not that I needed it, of course.

His daughter Kate Stewart became the Head of Scientific Research at UNIT. She's pretty brilliant, too. She did nearly blow up London to stop the Zygons, but that's UNIT for you!

My old mate Martha Jones worked for UNIT for a bit. She's got a big brain so they were desperate to make her their Medical Director. She helped me and Donna with some Sontaran problems.

My companions Liz Shaw, Jo Grant and Harry Sullivan were also from UNIT. They were called assistants, though. What's in a name?

HOW TO SPOT A UNIT SOLDIER!

THESE SOLDIERS AREN'T ALWAYS THE BRIGHTEST!

THEY WEAR RED BERETS. I DID ASK IF THEY HAD ANY FEZZES, BUT APPARENTLY NOT.

THEY WEAR THE UNIT INSIGNIA ON THEIR UNIFORM.

BLACK CLOTHES. VERY FLATTERING.

THINGS TO REMEMBER!

● You're the boss! Even though you do work for them. They might have guns – but you're in charge. In fact, even more reason to be in charge.

● They like to blow things up so keep them in line.

● Make sure they're respectful to aliens. They might be ugly, but they're not all bad. Neither are the aliens.

● They've got a secret stash of extraterrestrial tech called the Black Archive. This needs to be looked at.

● They have this thing called the Osterhagen Key – which basically blows up Earth if aliens invade.

TRY TO LOSE THAT.

HOW TO PLAY THE RECORDER!

IT'S IMPORTANT THAT YOU KNOW THAT WE ARE VERY MUSICAL! SO, GET PLAYING THIS RECORDER!

IT'S EASY TO PLAY!

JUST BLOW IN THIS BIT!

COVER THE BACK HOLE WITH YOUR THUMB AND THE TOP HOLE WITH YOUR INDEX FINGER. THAT'S A B!

NOW YOU'RE QUALIFIED. PLAY SOMETHING BY BEETHOVEN.

THIS IS MORE THAN A WOODWIND INSTRUMENT. IT'S ALSO:

● A great tool for helping you think

● Ideal for keeping you busy if you've been imprisoned

● Handy for destroying renegade Time Lords

KNOW YOUR JELLY BABIES!

YOU MIGHT FIND SOME JELLY BABIES IN SOME OF YOUR POCKETS, OR IN ALL OF YOUR POCKETS, BUT DON'T BE SCARED.

THESE JELLY BABIES NEED TO BE CONTROLLED. IMPRISON THEM IN A PAPER BAG TO RUIN ANY ESCAPE PLANS.

THEY'RE EASY TO EAT. PUT ONE IN YOUR MOUTH AND CHEW. DELICIOUS, NO?

BEFORE EXITING THE TARDIS THROW ONE IN THE AIR AND SEE IF IT FALLS TO THE FLOOR TO TEST THE GRAVITY OF UNEXPLORED PLANETS.

OFFER THEM TO ENEMIES. I OFFERED ONE TO DAVROS, BUT HE DECLINED. HE IS A MANIAC!

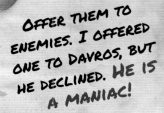

THESE ARE MORE THAN JUST SWEETS. THEY'RE ALSO:

- Good for making people think you eat real babies. As if!

- Suitable for making impeccable first impressions

- Good for confusing foes with weapons!

HOW TO EAT FISH FINGERS AND CUSTARD!

If you're going to be me, then you need to know how to eat like me. Think fun, think nutrition, think . . . fish fingers and custard.

THE DIRECT DIP

Perfect for beginners. Just pop your fish finger into the bowl of custard and remove.
And then eat.
And then go
'Mmm, tasty!'

THE FISHY FLICK

Hold the fish finger at an angle to ensure a quick and satisfying scoop. Perfect for those experimenting with custard-to-fish ratios.

THE DOUBLE DUNK

Dip as above, but then turn and dip the other side, too. Some call it madness. But hey, I am a madman with a box . . . of fish fingers.

THE SWIRL

Add the fish finger and, instead of dipping quickly, send the old fish finger for a spin around the bowl. A must for fans of fishy custard.

THE SANDWICH

A traditional fish finger sandwich – but with loads of custard between the bread. Everything is tons better when placed between two slices of bread. Except Sontarans.

LOVE FISH FINGERS AND CUSTARD? THEN TRY MY MENU MASH-UP!

SAUSAGES AND STRAWBERRY JAM

A wholesome meal for the sweet-toothed!

ICE CREAM WITH SPAGHETTI

Slimy, creamy and ever-so dreamy!

CELERY AND CHOCOLATE SPREAD

Crunchy and sweet for a munchy treat!

CORNFLAKES WITH CABBAGE

Cereal with heart!

RICE AND SPRINKLES

Rockin' rice that's extra nice! And rather beautiful. Marry me.

A GUIDE TO GROSS THINGS!

TRUST ME – YOU'LL NEED THIS GUIDE!

PARPS!

Do not get in the way of the Slitheen – but do not get behind them either, because we're talking about some seriously gross trumps!

ALIEN BOGIES!

Watch where you put your limbs. Get distracted for one second and you might dip your hands into some super-nasty snot!

HELLO, SMELL-O!

LIVING FLESH!

Not only is this Ganger-making goo totally slippy and slimy, it's pretty dangerous. And you will not be able to wash it out of your tweed blazer.

OOD SPIT!

Possessed Ood have red eyes. They also get foamy tentacles and can spray your face with their frond foam. Urgh! Say it, don't spray it.

HOW TO USE YOUR CELERY!

DON'T UNDERESTIMATE THIS SIMPLE VEGETABLE. WELL, YOU CAN IF YOU WANT. I DON'T MIND.

IF THIS TURNS PURPLE THEN THERE ARE GASES PRESENT IN THE PRAXIS RANGE OF THE SPECTRUM. THIS IS BAD NEWS BECAUSE YOU'RE ALLERGIC TO THEM!

UH-OH!

PIN THIS ON TO YOUR JACKET. WHY? BECAUSE IT LOOKS AWESOME, THAT'S WHY!

FEELING PECKISH? THEN HAVE A NIBBLE.

THIS IS MORE THAN JUST A VEGETABLE.
IT CAN ALSO BE USED AS:

● A mini broom – if you turn it upside down and give it to a mouse

● A way to wake up companions, if they're the sort of creature woken up by the smell of celery

● An emergency toothbrush

127

HOW TO SPOT ALIENS IN DISGUISE!

YOU'RE GOING TO NEED TO KNOW THIS!

Humans are a pretty odd lot, so working out which ones are monsters in disguise can be tough work. Follow these tips and you'll be very nearly, kind of, almost, sorted!

SLITHEEN

THESE RAXACORICOFALLAPATORIANS ARE ALWAYS UP TO SOMETHING. IF THEY'RE ON EARTH THEN THEY'LL BE DISGUISED AS HUMANS.

They're totally Slitheen!

They'll track down a larger person, skin them and then use their compression collars to help them fit in the skin suit.

Not as cool as a bow tie!

WATCH OUT FOR:

- Zips in the forehead. A total giveaway! Good place for a pencil case.

- Bad tempers and a desire to take over the world.

- Parps! Parps! Parps! Compressing a big alien into a tight skin suit can create stinking trumps.

DALEK PUPPETS

DALEKS ARE THE DEADLIEST AND MOST DEVIOUS CREATURES IN THE UNIVERSE, SO DON'T BE SURPRISED TO SEE ONE IN HUMAN FORM!

THAT'S GOTTA HURT!

She's not human!

Daleks will target specific people to transform - not just enemies, but those who have access to their enemies.

This one went after Amy Pond!

Hmmm, this disguise needs work!

WATCH OUT FOR:

- Buzzing lights! These horror hybrids give off strange vibes!

- Cold hands. And cold everything else. Basically, they're dead and taken over by the Dalek nanocloud.

- The biggest giveaway is the eyestalk sticking out of the forehead.

ZYGONS

ALL THE WAY FROM ZYGOR, THESE SHAPE-SHIFTING, SUCKER-COVERED MONSTERS ARE THE MASTERS OF DISGUISE.

Zygons can **take the shape of anyone!** They target influential and powerful people.

They can even take on the shapes of animals.

WATCH OUT FOR:

- Venomous tongue sacs - keep clear of their mouths. Absolutely no kissing!

- Gross goo! Any slime lying around could be the Zygons' organic technology.

- Human doubles! Zygons have to keep their victims alive to maintain the shape-shift.

That's put me off my biscuits!

SATURNYNES

Did someone say fish from space? Never mind the smell, you'll know something fishy is going on when you spot their fangs. And when they try to drain your blood!

SPOONHEADS

These walking servers have one purpose - to upload you to the Cloud. They'll repeat your words - and watch out for swivelling hollow heads!

THE FAMILY OF BLOOD

This terrifying family of hunters can take over humans. They can be recognized by their scarecrow servants and the strange way they talk to each other. It's all 'son-of-mine' and 'mother-of-yours' and all that.

WHY BOW TIES ARE COOL!

IT WOULD BE MUCH QUICKER IF I HAD TO LIST WHY THEY AREN'T COOL – BUT IN CASE YOU'RE ONE OF THOSE DIFFICULT REGENERATION TYPES, **HERE GOES!**

They look awesome. Super-smart!

They give you an air of authority. If you've been blessed with a baby face (and it doesn't happen often), you'll need something distinguished to wear.

You can't go to a posh do or board the starship Titanic in any old tie.

They can be used to tie around door handles to stop ghosties getting you.

They complement tweed beautifully.

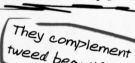

They look a bit like butterflies. Now, we know that butterflies are evil aliens set on taking over Earth, but humans seem to think they're pretty.

They're cool because they're not cool. Which makes them cool. Cool?

HOW TO USE YOUR UMBRELLA

IF YOU WANT AN UMBRELLA, THERE'S ONE IN THE TARDIS WARDROBE. ROW 67292, SHELF 48376262, SECTION ALPHA-SPAGHETTI-SOAP. JUST BEFORE THE UNICORN AND THE UNICYCLE.

STEP 1

Hold it by the handle to keep it close. Ideal for pointing.

LOOK! AN ALIEN!

STEP 2

If it rains normal rain, hold it up and open it. Perfect. If it's acid rain you might want to run.

STEP 3

Keep it ready in case you have to face any monsters with swords. En garde!

STEP 4

When hanging off ledges, hold the main part of the umbrella and hook the handle onto something secure.

STEP 5

Turn it upside down and fill it with water for a portable birdbath or dinosaur drinking cup. (Do not forget to take the birds out first).

HOW TO STOP ALIEN INVASIONS!

ALIENS SIMPLY **LOVE** INVADING PLANETS. ESPECIALLY EARTH, WHICH IS QUITE FUNNY BECAUSE IT SMELLS A BIT LIKE CHIPS. HERE ARE SOME TOP TIPS ON STOPPING INVASIONS OF EARTH.

IF THE ALIENS WANT TO ENSLAVE THE HUMANS . . .

Simply hide them away in cellars or in trees and then leave a note out for the aliens saying 'Sorry! <u>We got bored and went to live on the Lost Moon of Poosh</u>!'

NO HUMANS **HERE.** APOLOGIES.

IF THE ALIENS WANT TO HARVEST EARTH'S MINERALS . . .

Organize a sample of Earth soil, but replace it with jelly. Send it to the aliens and they'll go home in a grump. Unless they really like jelly. In that case, destroy all jelly.

IF THE ALIENS JUST WANT TO BLOW EARTH UP . . .

Take a trip to the alien ship and politely request that they back off. If they refuse, tinker with the ship's circuits so they can only reverse away and they have no hot water.

IF THE ALIENS WANT TO EAT THE HUMANS . . .

Get loads of cactuses and put wigs on them. Then say, 'Oh, hi! These are the humans. You can eat them if you want, but they're very prickly.' Works a treat.

IF THE ALIENS WANT TO TURN EARTH INTO A CLONE COLONY . . .

I'm thinking of Sontarans here. They like to try to poison the atmosphere so they can turn it into a clone planet. Get a GIANT fan to blow their dirty air away.

IF THE ALIENS TRY TO STEAL EARTH . . .

It's happened before – it could happen again. Try tethering Earth down with a big anchor, so it's far too heavy to be shifted away. Ha. Beat that, Davros!

GUIDE TO AWESOME GADGETS!

EVERYTHING YOU NEED TO KNOW ABOUT THE TOP TECH I KEEP IN THE **TARDIS!**

SONIC SCREWDRIVER

Seriously – keep this with you at all times, unless you think you can pick locks without it.

You can't.

HAS OVER 2,500 SETTINGS!

USES SOUNDWAVES. NEAT, HUH?

HOLD IT HERE – SO YOU DON'T BURN YOUR FINGERS!

PRIMARY EMITTER CLUSTER (GLOWY BIT)

NEW PSYCHIC INTERFACE – JUST POINT AND THINK!

USE IT FOR:

- Opening doors
- Scanning tech and organic matter
- Accessing computer systems
- Acting as a nifty microphone

WARNING!

- The sonic doesn't do wood!
- It can't open anything that has been deadlocked!
- Keep it away from certain hairdryers. Ka-boom!

SUPER SONICS!

KEEP YOUR EYES PEELED FOR THESE OTHER SONICS FROM OUR PAST.

NOT EXACTLY SUBTLE, BUT THEN I DID OPERATE THIS WHEN WEARING A CAPE.

SORT OF A RE-FIT, BUT I WAS FOND OF IT.

PRETTY BASIC AND RED AND GLOWY. USED IN VERY UN-DOCTORISH WAYS.

USED BY OUR NINTH AND TENTH INCARNATIONS — THIS IS PRETTY NIFTY, BUT A LITTLE SMALL!

HAS DAMPERS, A RED SETTING AND A NEURAL RELAY. VERY IMPORTANT, THAT LAST ONE.

FUTURE SONIC

I've been thinking about a new design.

Huge! With more apps – can even do wood!

Mega-glowy primary emitter cluster

Custard supply nozzle

TIMEY-WIMEY DETECTOR

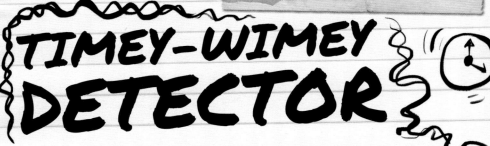

LOOKING FOR TIME DISTURBANCES CREATED BY THE WEEPING ANGELS? THEN YOU'RE GOING TO NEED THIS!

Now, I had to make this when the Weeping Angels sent Martha and me back in time.

It's made from bits and pieces of everyday things from the sixties, like a kettle and a radio.

To use it – just point it around an area, and when it finds something timey-wimey, like someone blasted into the past by a Weeping Angel, it goes DING!

GOES DING HERE! I LOVE THAT NOISE!

HOLD IT BY THIS HANDLE HERE!

EVERY TIMEY-WIMEY DEVICE NEEDS A CLOCK

TELEPHONE!

WARNING!
THIS THING BOILS AN EGG AT THIRTY PACES. MIGHT SOUND HANDY. NOT IF YOU'RE A CHICKEN. SORRY, LADIES!

138

VORTEX MANIPULATOR

NEED TO TRAVEL THROUGH TIME, BUT YOU DON'T HAVE A TARDIS? THEN, DON'T USE THIS — IT'S RUBBISH! SORRY, CAPTAIN JACK!

HANDY FOR TELEPORTING

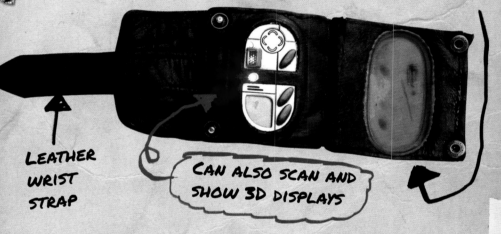

LEATHER WRIST STRAP

CAN ALSO SCAN AND SHOW 3D DISPLAYS

This time-hopping device was created by the Time Agents in the fifty-first century for going backwards and forwards in time!

It's a cheap and nasty form of time travel that uses Time Vortex energy to work. It's bumpier than riding a camel on a cobbled street. And I should know.

This needs a special code to work – and I know it! Jack doesn't! I'll write it down somewhere safe for you!

Although a bit choppy, it's come in handy and me, Jack, River and Clara have all used it to save our skins! Try to avoid using it, though.

VISUAL RECOGNITION SYSTEM

NEED TO IDENTIFY AN ALIEN PRONTO? THEN THIS IS THE GADGET YOU NEED. SHAME IT'S NOT SMALLER OR NICER OR BETTER

MINI STEERING HANDLES

INTERNAL POWER SUPPLY

FOR SEEING BEHIND YOU

This was a <u>gift from a two-headed godmother.</u> I thought it was useless. <u>A real pile of junk.</u> I was wrong. I'll say sorry to both heads.

It came in handy for identifying an invisible alien called a Krafayis, that caused some trouble for Vincent Van Gogh.

Just point the mirror at the alien of your choice and await the handy print-out that will name the species and place of origin of the creature.

PSYCHIC PAPER

VERY HANDY WHEN YOU
WANT TO PRETEND YOU
ARE SOMEONE ELSE!

HANDY HOLDER

PAPER THAT'S PSYCHIC.

This is your pass to everywhere! Simply think what you want it to display and whoever you show it to will see whatever you want it to say. It's a universal ID.

It can also receive messages from people with strong telepathic ability.

WARNING! MAKE SURE YOU KNOW WHAT YOU'RE THINKING. YOU DON'T WANT ANY OLD NONSENSE SHOWING UP ON THE PAPER.

WARNING! SOME SPECIAL, EXTRA-CLEVER PEOPLE LIKE US AND SHAKESPEARE COULD SEE RIGHT THROUGH IT. TORCHWOOD STAFF ARE TRAINED TO SEE IT TOO.

HERE ARE A FEW NAMES I'VE USED WITH THE PSYCHIC PAPER: John Smith. Proconsul. Sherlock Holmes. Dr James McCrimmon. Sir Doctor of TARDIS.

HOW TO FLY MY TARDIS!

FLYING THE OLD GIRL IS EASY, REALLY. BUT IT'LL PROBABLY BE THE FIRST THING YOU FORGET. THIS GUIDE SHOULD GET YOU STARTED, BECAUSE I AM, AFTER ALL, AN EXPERT.

Want to send time co-ordinates and other important controlly sort of data to the rest of the TARDIS? Then start here. Good for outgoing communications such as text messages. LOL.

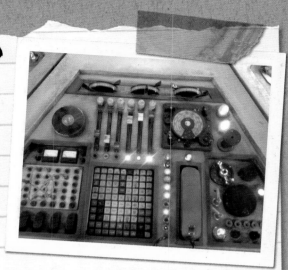

This directly controls the TARDIS engines and allows you to manually steer the TARDIS if, for example, you spill a strawberry milkshake over everything.

This super-swanky panel allows you to directly connect with the mind of the TARDIS. Do not think EXPLODE! EXPLODE! EXPLODE! Oh, you are now, sorry.

This is where information is received. It can be displayed on the screens above the console. Very handy for watching DVDs, should you ever wish to.

The **auxiliary** <u>**power control**</u> acts as a <u>**back-up**</u> for <u>**all of the other**</u> <u>**systems**</u>. It also has some flickering lights. I'm not sure what they do, but I could watch them for hours.

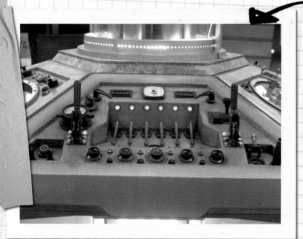

Now, if it all starts going a bit wrong, this panel right here is for you. It's for **manual adjustments** to the time co-ordinates. Ideal for when everything else has **exploded**.

DESKTOP DESIGNS

UNFORTUNATELY THE CHAMELEON CIRCUIT IS STILL BROKEN, SO THE OUTSIDE SHAPE OF THE *TARDIS* WILL NOT BE CHANGING ANY TIME SOON. HOWEVER, YOU CAN GET PRETTY CREATIVE WITH THE INTERIOR

How cool is this? Spinning bits! Flashing bits! I'm pretty happy with how this is at the moment. I suspect you will be too. I'm sure you won't want to change a thing . . .

YOU KNOW HOW TO USE THIS NOW. WELL DONE, YOU.

THIS IS THE POWER CONTROL. KEEP IT ON, I SAY!

RAILS — JUST IN CASE THINGS GET BUMPY. (THEY WILL!)

SHOULD YOU WISH, THIS WOULD BE THE PERFECT PLACE FOR A HAT STAND.

I LOVE A WALKWAY. PERFECT FOR MAKING A REAL ENTRANCE.

Other interesting recent designs include:

THE STEAM PUNK

I USED TO LOVE WATCHING THE TIME ROTOR BOBBING UP AND DOWN.

VERY BRASSY. LOOKS GREAT, BUT I HAD TO GET AN OOD IN TO POLISH IT.

VERY COMFORTABLE. EVEN CONSOLE ROOMS NEED CHAIRS SOMETIMES.

THE CRAZY CORAL

JUST FOR A CHANGE FROM ROUNDELS, I WENT WITH HEXAGONS!

VERY GLOWY AND GREEN. ALMOST SPOOKY, SOME WOULD SAY. NOT ME.

THIS CONSOLE ROOM HAD A VERY ORGANIC CORAL THEME. I REDECORATED. I DIDN'T LIKE IT.

TOP TARDIS TIPS!

KEEP AN EYE ON THIS BULB. LAST TIME IT NEEDED CHANGING IT WAS PRETTY TOUGH TO DO.

FORGOT YOUR KEY? THEN JUST CLICK YOUR FINGERS TO OPEN THE DOOR!

YES, LIKE I SAID, IT GOT STUCK LIKE THIS POLICE BOX IN THE 1950s. I'M RATHER FOND OF IT, THOUGH.

IDRIS

The TARDIS Matrix once entered a human form called Idris. She was bright, clever, fun and as mad as a box of frogs. She got past, present and future mixed up and liked biting.

TIME ZOMBIES

There was a slight problem with a magno-grab snatching the TARDIS when it was in basic mode. Long story short, the engines nearly blew up and there were Time Zombies on the loose.

MY PHOTO ALBUM

NOW, JUST TO MAKE SURE THAT WE DON'T LOSE THE ESSENTIAL MEMORIES – HERE ARE A FEW PHOTOS AND BITS I'VE BEEN KEEPING HOLD OF.

ADVANCED QUANTUM MECHANICS

A very pretty warning!

YAY! I FOUND A GOLDEN TICKET!

HEDGEWICKS WORLD

GOLDEN TICKET

ADMITS 4

149

ood
operations

new price cut
only 50 credits
BUY ONE NOW

ood
operations

Service
with a
smile

A LETTER FROM THE MISSUS!

TITANIC

A NOT VERY
LUXURIOUS
CRUISE.

THIS WAS ONE JOB
I DID NOT WANT!

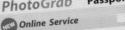

SAY CHEESE, CLARA!

БРЕД ОДИН... ИЗ НАС... И ВЫ ВРЕДИТ ВСЕМ НАМ!

Big FRIENDLY BUTTON

LOVE THOSE FRONDS, BUDDY!

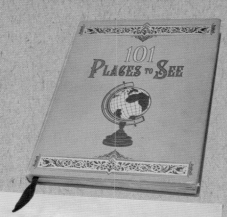

101 PLACES TO SEE

RUN YOU CLEVER BOY AND REMEMBER

THE GREAT INTELLIGENCE INSTITUTE
2 BLOOMSBURY LANE • LONDON N31

HOW DID THAT GET HERE?

Save the weeping Angel.

THE PONDS!

NOT ALL MEMORIES CAN
BE ONES YOU WANT.

ATMOS

NO, THANK YOU!

MY QUICK GUIDE!

LIFE IS CONFUSING AND NOT EVERYONE IS AS CLEVER AS ME, SO HERE IS A CONVENIENT PAGE OF NIFTY REFERENCES.

POTATO DWARF = STRAX

HUSH = EVERYONE BE QUIET. I AM TALKING!

OLD GIRL = **THE TARDIS**

BUTTERFLIES = **EVIL ALIENS** INTENT ON TAKING OVER THE WORLD

BOW TIES, FEZZES, STETSONS = **COOL**

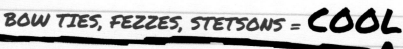

NO! = NO, **NO**, **NO!**

FISH FROM SPACE = VAMPIRES

POND = AMY. OR RORY. OR MELODY. OR BRIAN.

MRS ROBINSON = RIVER SONG

THINGS I CAN DO!

JUST FOR YOUR RECORDS, I CAN DO THESE, SO YOU CAN TOO!

Speak five billion different languages! Including Baby, Horse and Cat!

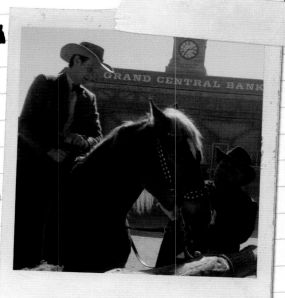

You can read and write Old High Gallifreyan!

You can smell and taste exactly what time things are from. Handy.

You've got a nifty photographic memory, which can remember all sorts of details!

Invent amazing food. Hello, Yorkshire Puddings!

You can make cheese! We have a doctorate in cheese-making.

You're still learning to knit.

TIME LORD
TECHNOLOGY

RASSILON'S GAUNTLET

The Lord President of the Time Lords was in possession of a weapon that only someone of his experience and wisdom should control. This ancient and powerful gauntlet can be used to destroy deserters and traitors by emitting an energy bolt that flashes from the weapon.

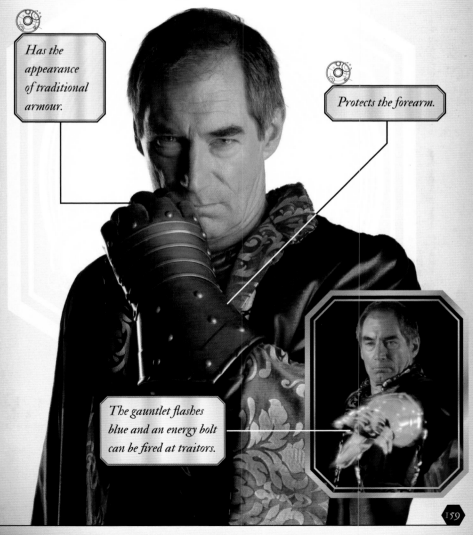

Has the appearance of traditional armour.

Protects the forearm.

The gauntlet flashes blue and an energy bolt can be fired at traitors.

PSYCHIC CONTAINER

These emergency messaging devices can carry psychic notices from one Time Lord to another. They are equipped to travel through time and space. They can withstand the Time Vortex and deliver thoughts to alert others of danger. The containers often carry markers to show who the message is from.

Contains Time Lord information.

Can travel through time and space.

Appears as an illuminated box.

I got sent one!

CHAMELEON ARCH

This device can rewrite every cell in a Time Lord's body to turn them into a new species. Used within their TARDIS, the Time Lord's biology will change and they will be provided with a lifetime of memories so they believe they are that species. Their true essence will be stored within the fob watch, and must be kept safe at all costs.

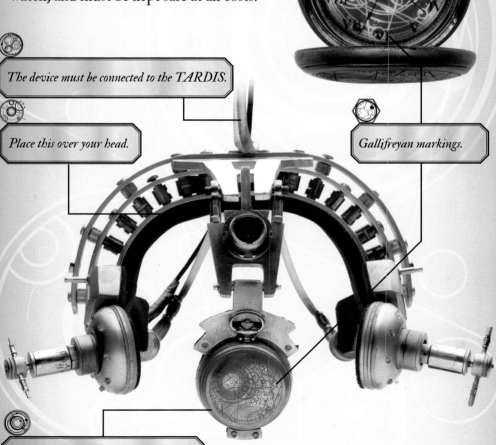

The device must be connected to the TARDIS.

Place this over your head.

Gallifreyan markings.

The fob watch must be placed here.

GENESIS ARK

The Genesis Ark is a Dalek prison ship created by the Time Lords. Like so much of our superior technology, it is dimensionally transcendental, or 'bigger on the inside', as some uneducated humans have said. This prison can only be opened by the touch of a Time Lord or time-traveller, as it requires Artron energy to bring it out of hibernation. Daleks do not have hands and therefore can't open it themselves.

The prison ship is the shape of a Dalek.

Can only be activated by the touch of a time-traveller.

This prison hovers, and if evacuated requires a space of over thirty square miles.

Artron handprint will glow before the prison ship opens.

THE MOMENT

Created by the Ancients of Gallifrey, this is the most powerful device in the universe. It is stored as a forbidden weapon, within the Omega arsenal in the Time Vaults. This weapon is so sophisticated that it has a living interface, which can take the form of someone important from your timeline. It acts as a conscience and forces you to explore all possible outcomes.

Has a sentient operating system.

Pressing this button was one of the hardest decisons I've ever had to make!

Produces an activation button, if required.

Can open time fissures and access time-locked events.

TIME LORD
MYTHS AND LEGENDS

For a species as intelligent as the Time Lords, you may not think that there would be much need for story-telling – for we create the myths and we are the legends. However, stories carry morals and meanings and are ideal for sharing traditions. They are also useful for connecting with lesser beings such as humans.

THE TOCLAFANE

The Toclafane is known as 'the bogeyman' of Gallifrey. It is a mysterious creature that haunts our dreams and hides within the shadows. The term 'Toclafane' is used to address all manner of supernatural creatures thought to reside on Gallifrey and is a collective description for anything sinister or chilling. Many young Gallifreyans a

Well, they became real, thanks to the Master! When the last of humanity cannibalized themselves and became cyborgs, he used a paradox machine to send them back to Earth to destroy themselves. He gave them the most frightening name he could think of –

THE TOCLAFANE.

THE SHAKRI

There is no greater legend than that of the Shakri. Time Lord mythology states that the powerful Shakri could exist in all places at once and that they held magnificent power. They were believed to travel in groups of seven, and a transcript that was discovered, with several other ancient psy

YUP!

THEY'RE REAL, TOO.

They're not mystical angels. They're just pest-controllers, zapping certain species to stop them becoming too numerous.
It's not their decision. They plant cubes on planets so they can investigate the inhabitants - in order to find out how to kill them.

TERRIBLE
BEHAVIOUR.

THE RHYME OF RASSILON'S TOWER

Who unto Rassilon's Tower will go,
must choose above, between, below.

THE THREE LITTLE SONTARANS

This children's classic has proven to be a popular story for generations.
The tale follows the fortunes of three little Sontarans as they embark on a
mission that teaches them an important life lesson. One must not forget that
Sontarans are a threat to Gallifrey, and that there is very little humour to be
found in them.

I DON'T KNOW ABOUT THAT!

Meet my mate Strax and you'll see what I mean.

TIME LORD RULES

— DO —

- Act with dignity at all times.

- Wear appropriate Time Lord dress that does not rely on accessories.

- Swear to protect the planet Gallifrey at any cost.

- Make sure that your body is disposed of, should you die and run out of regenerations.

- Remain cautious about travel between parallel worlds.

DO HAVE AS MUCH **FUN** AS POSSIBLE!

DO SEE EVERY SINGLE CORNER AND NOOK AND PIXEL OF TIME AND SPACE!

DO INVENT WEIRD FOODS AND GADGETS!

— DON'T —

- Interfere with time.

- Invite humans or other species in general into your TARDIS for extended periods.

- Mix unusual forms of alien food. Freeze-dried pills are more effective.

- Run. Stand proudly as a Time Lord.

- Attempt to extend your life further through science or Time Lord mythology.

- Commit any act which destroys an entire species.

DON'T BE BORING!

DON'T WEAR LOTS OF RED CAPES AND FLASHY COLLARS!

DON'T PUNISH ANYONE FOR HELPING!

FIND YOUR
TIME LORD
NAME

A Time Lord must have a strong name that represents their power, status and beliefs. Those who are not allotted a name or nickname during their time at the Time Lord Academy can use these charts to find a title.

USE THE FIRST LETTER
OF YOUR FIRST NAME TO
DISCOVER WHAT YOUR
TITLE OR INTRODUCTION
SHOULD BE:

A–F = PROFESSOR

G–L = THE

M–R = LORD

S–Z = GRAND

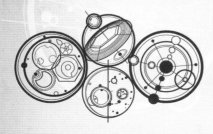

NOW, TAKE THE FIRST LETTER OF YOUR SURNAME TO LEARN YOUR MAIN TIME LORD NAME.

A = Venturer

B = Saint

C = Winner

D = Explorer

E = Shield

F = Infinite

G = Challenger

H = Meteor

I = Protector

J = Vortron

K = Athlete

L = Zenarck

M = Dimensioneer

N = Golven

O = Immortal

P = Dynamo

Q = Shadow

R = Pioneer

S = Force

T = Champion

U = Voyager

V = Typhoon

W = Dextive

X = Moorid

Y = Cosmos

Z = Defender

MY TIME LORD NAME IS:

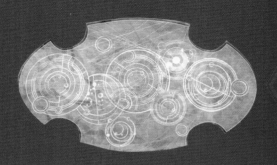

TIME LORD
PLEDGE

TIME LORD
CERTIFICATION

*By studying this official text and
learning the lessons of our graceful
and powerful kind, you are now
ready to become a Time Lord.*

I UNDERSTAND THE IMPORTANCE OF MY SACRED POSITION

I WILL NOT MEDDLE WITH TIME

I WILL RESPECT THE TRADITIONS OF GALLIFREY

COMPLETE YOUR CERTIFICATE BY WRITING AND SIGNING YOUR NAMES:

WRITE YOUR TIME LORD NAME HERE:

WRITE YOUR REAL NAME HERE:

SIGN YOUR REAL NAME HERE:

Doctor's CERTIFICATE

Nearly anyone can be a **TIME LORD**, but you – you have to be like me, the **DOCTOR**. There's more fun, more running and a whole heap more dipping tasty things into even tastier things to create mega-tasty things.

Being the Doctor is a **HUGE RESPONSIBILITY.** You have to help and heal and have fun.

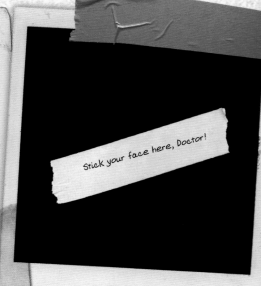

Stick your face here, Doctor!

If you can tick the boxes below, then you're ready to take the name of the Doctor.

- [ ] I understand **RULE NUMBER ONE** - the Doctor lies.

- [ ] I will always try my hardest to be good.

- [ ] Basically, I will keep on **RUNNING**!

- [ ] I'll be as brave and clever as I can be.

OK, now write your name here:

And sign here:

GERONIMO!